Snow White

Snow White

Retold by
JOYCE DUNBAR

Illustrated by
JULIE MONKS

SCHOLASTIC
PRESS

For my dear friend, Christine Bolland
J.D.

For Phyllis Bligh
J.M.

Scholastic Children's Books
Commonwealth House, 1-19 New Oxford Street
London WC1A 1NU, UK
a division of Scholastic Ltd
London ~ New York ~ Toronto ~ Sydney ~ Auckland
Mexico City ~ New Delhi ~ Hong Kong

First published in hardback in the UK by Scholastic Ltd, 2005

You can visit Joyce Dunbar's website: www.joycedunbar.com

*I*ntroduction

Three drops of blood upon the snow, a magic mirror, a poisoned apple, scorching slippers: *Snow White* gleams with vivid images and a subtle wintry beauty. It is one of the darker tales from Grimm: about child abandonment, attempted murder, sorcery and enchantment. But above all it is about the destructive power of jealousy, showing a woman at the mercy of a raging emotion that ultimately brings about her downfall. The Queen is wonderfully, fascinatingly, picturesquely, appallingly wicked.

But it is the redeeming power of the fairy tale that prevails. Truth wins over falsehood, love over hatred, good over evil. The princess gets her prince.

So, why add to the original? For me, it was a chance, not so much to elaborate, as to explore. What was it really like for a princess to be looking after seven little men? Why did she disobey the obviously sound advice of the dwarfs? How did the Queen go back and forth over seven mountains?

It has been a huge pleasure for me to ponder these questions, to be one of the legion of storytellers to render their version of this bewitching tale.

Joyce Dunbar

Long ago in the middle of winter, a queen sat sewing at her window. The snow was falling in soft feathery flakes; beyond was the dark forest. The snow began to settle, forming a white blanket so that it seemed as if the whole world had gone into a deep and silent sleep.

"How beautiful the white snow is against the black ebony of the window frame," mused the Queen. She was so lost in thought that she accidentally pricked her finger with her needle.

Three drops of blood fell upon the snow.

"Ah," sighed the Queen, "if only I had a child like this, with skin as white as snow, hair as black as ebony and lips as red as blood. Then I might remember this moment forever."

Not long after, the Queen gave birth to a baby daughter.

"Her skin is as white as snow," said the first nurse in attendance.

"Her hair is as black as ebony," said the second nurse.

"Her lips are as red as blood," said the third.

"Her name shall be Snow White," whispered the Queen.

But alas, as the Queen cradled the child in her arms for the first time, so at that moment, she died.

The King was heartbroken: a birth to celebrate and a death to mourn! He fell into a deep melancholy but he realised that his daughter needed a mother, so after a year he began to look for another wife. In his own kingdom not a woman could be found to match the beauty of his former wife, so he began to look further afield. Ambassadors from far off lands came with portraits of foreign princesses, but the reality always disappointed.

The King sat upon his throne, weary with despair. "No more portraits," he said. "I have seen enough."

"You haven't seen this one," came a voice from the throng of courtiers.

"Who spoke?" said the King. "Who dared to speak without permission?"

Stepping forward was a figure veiled in purple from head to foot. The King looked at what was held before him.

"That is no portrait," he said. "That is a mirror."

To the King's astonishment, it was the mirror that answered:

"Look into my depths,
Conjure your heart's desire.
Summon your wildest dreams,
Feel love burn like a fire."

When the King looked into the mirror he saw, not his own reflection, but an image of a woman more beautiful than he had ever dreamed of. "She shall be my queen," he said. "Where shall I find her?"

With that the purple veil fell away and the woman stood before him in the fullness of her beauty. The King was spellbound. Never had he seen such eyes of forest green, such burnished copper hair, such flawless olive skin. In barely a week they were married.

But just as the new Queen was beautiful, so she was vain and haughty. Seven maids attended her, bathing, dressing, grooming, painting, plucking, clipping, polishing, so that she never looked less than perfect. And because she had a jealous eye, she made sure that all of her maids were plain.

She soon began to cast her eyes around the court to make sure there was no one to rival her. There was, possibly, one – but she was too young to matter. "What a pretty thing your daughter is," she said to the King. "I shall try to look after her as her own mother might have."

"Yes, she is very pretty," said the King, scooping Snow White up in his arms and doing a little dance with her. "Who knows, one day she might grow up to be as beautiful as my first wife, who was queen before you."

What a poison dart this was in the Queen's heart! She didn't want to know about the beauty of another wife, another queen, only about her own.

Hidden in her chamber was the magic mirror that had so entranced the King. Every day the Queen looked at herself in this mirror, searching its depths, and asked,

"Mirror, mirror, on the wall,

Who is the fairest one of all?"

The mirror always had the same answer:

"You, O Queen, are the fairest of all."

Then the Queen was satisfied. She knew the mirror could only speak the truth and that she had nothing to fear from Snow White.

"Pretty thing," she cooed, petting and playing with the young Princess. But behind her smile there was danger; in her forest-green eyes there was a glint. Poison seeped from her heart.

Day by day, night by night, Snow White grew more beautiful. Her black hair shone like jet, her white skin was as creamy as milk, her red lips as sweet as a rose. Her nature was sweet, too. The shyest of birds in the garden would eat from her hands, the most timid of the forest fawns came to her for a nuzzle. She charmed everyone who met her.

All except her father. So besotted was he by his new queen that he paid less and less attention to his daughter. He even forgot her birthdays, so that Snow White began to forget them herself.

One day, when Snow White was seven years old, the Queen looked as usual into her magic mirror and asked,

"Mirror, mirror, on the wall,

Who is the fairest one of all?"

But this time, for the first time, the mirror gave a different answer:

"You, O Queen, are wondrous fair,

But Snow White beyond compare."

The Queen turned green with envy. Her eyes blazed. Her hair crackled with spite. How she hated Snow White. She knew that as the

little Princess blossomed, so would her own beauty fade. But not if she had her way. She wanted to be the most beautiful, and forever.

Like a weed, envy grew in the Queen's heart, squeezing out any goodness that was there. Hatred hardened her eyes and pinched her mouth, which made her ugly, which made her angry, which made her uglier still, until she was in quite a frenzy. And who was the cause of all this? Snow White! And what did she have to do? Destroy her!

She sent for a huntsman and said, "Take the child into the forest, kill her and bring her heart to me as proof that you have done what I have ordered."

The huntsman set out with Snow White into the forest with a grievous spirit. He did not want to kill Snow White. He had known her since she was an infant, and would often take her into the forest to show her some baby fox cubs or a young deer. But he had to obey the Queen or pay with his own life. Deeper and deeper into the forest they went until it began to get dark.

Snow White had no idea of the danger she was in. "Look at the fireflies," she said. "See how they glow in the dark."

Even so, she felt tired. "Dear friend," she said at last, "why are we going so far? It will soon be nightfall and we will be unable to find our way home."

"Not much further now, Princess," he replied.

The huntsman led her into the deepest part of the forest, until at last he came to a halt. "That's it," he urged. "Just keep watching the fireflies."

He seized his knife, sweating and trembling at the thought of what he was about to do. At that moment Snow White turned and saw the knife raised in his hand. She saw the terrible expression on his face.

"Poor huntsman," she said. "I can see that you're afraid. Don't be. The wild beasts will not hurt you. They have never hurt me."

Her innocence melted the heart of the huntsman and he fell to his knees. "Forgive me for the dreadful deed I almost carried out," he said. "Your stepmother, the Queen, ordered me to kill you. I cannot. But if I return with you alive I shall myself be killed. So I must leave you to find your own way."

With that, the huntsman slipped away, leaving Snow White alone in the forest. "The wild beasts will get her, however safe she may feel," he said to himself, "but at least her blood will not be on my hands." With an arrow he killed a wild deer, before cutting out its heart and returning to the palace.

"Here," he said, handing over his gruesome trophy. "All that is left of Snow White."

The Queen cooked it, and ate it, and rejoiced.

ow Snow White was afraid; afraid because her stepmother wanted to kill her, afraid to be alone in the forest. She stumbled along, tripping over tree roots, tumbling into fox holes. Bark scratched her skin. Brambles tore her clothes and her hair. Thistle and thorn prickled and stung her. Darker and darker, closer and closer, the forest loomed. It seemed to her the very trees were alive and would take hold of her and devour her. The further she went, the more lost she became. Even the light of the moon was hidden by a cloud, and the stars had lost their shine. It was utter, unfriendly darkness.

A wolf howled, driving Snow White one way. An owl screeched, startling her in another direction. A bat swooped, scaring her along a winding path. On and on she went, for what seemed like forever and a day.

Then – what did she see? A little clearing in the forest, and there, set back, nestling in a garden full of beautiful plants, a wooden house with a veranda. Here, seven little lanterns glowed in the night-time, shining from seven little windows.

Snow White tapped on the door. There was no answer. So tired and hungry was she that she overcame her fear and stepped inside.

She blinked in the gloom. Then, as her vision cleared, she saw that she was in the cosiest little house that gleamed and shone with copper and brass. Earthen pots and stone crocks stood about and glass jars glistened with the colour of jewels. Whoever lived here was very house proud! There was a fire all ready to be lit and in the centre was a scrubbed wooden table laid out with seven knives, seven forks, seven spoons. There were seven little bowls with food all ready to eat, and seven goblets full of wine. There were seven chairs around the table, with seven cushions. It was all so inviting, because it was all so small and homely.

"This food is not meant for me," thought Snow White. All the same, she could not help taking a tiny morsel of food from each bowl and a tiny sip of wine from each goblet. After that she felt drowsy.

In another room she found seven little beds with seven quilts. She climbed into the first bed.

"This one is too hard," she said to herself.

"This one is too soft," she said of the second bed.

"This one is too high," she said of the third.

"This one is too short," she said of the fourth.

"This one is too squeaky," she said of the fifth.

"This one is too low," she said of the sixth.

"This one is just right," she said of the seventh, and fell asleep.

A little while later there was a stomping of boots on the veranda – seven pairs of boots! They belonged to seven dwarfs, who had come home after long hours of toiling in the mountains, mining for precious gold and jewels.

They sensed something strange straightaway.

"My chair has been moved," said one.

"My fork is in the wrong place," said another.

"My spoon has been licked," said a third.

"My bread has been nibbled," said a fourth.

"My vegetables have been tasted," said a fifth.

"My knife has been used," said a sixth.

"There's a dribble on my goblet," said a seventh.

They took their seven lanterns from the windows and went into the bedroom to search.

"Someone has lain on my quilt," said one.

"Someone has dented my pillow," said another.

"Someone has crumpled my sheets," said a third.

"Someone has rumpled my nightshirt," said a fourth.

"Someone has tried on my nightcap," said a fifth.

"Someone has shuffled my slippers," said a sixth.

But when they came to the seventh bed they saw Snow White fast asleep and as comfortable as can be.

Their lanterns made a circle of light around her. Seven faces peered down in amazement.

"What is she?" asked one.

"An angel?" queried another.

"A fairy?" wondered another.

"She's a human," said a fourth.

"Did you ever see hair so black?" said a fifth.

"Or skin so white?" said a sixth.

"Or lips so red?" said the seventh.

"Or a creature so beautiful?" they murmured.

"She must have got lost in the forest," they agreed. "She surely can mean us no harm."

They were so delighted that they left her undisturbed. The seventh dwarf slept an hour at the end of the bed of each of his companions, till day began to dawn.

In the morning when Snow White awoke, she saw that the six little beds had been slept in. But by whom? And where were they? Would they be fierce, or friendly? She was wondering whether to climb out of the window or hide under the bed, when from the kitchen she heard such a gentle humming and murmuring, such a comforting hustle and bustle, that she was soothed into feeling safe.

She put her head round the door and saw seven little men, not so tall as herself, laying out the table for breakfast. Only this time there were eight places, not seven.

"Don't be afraid, my dear," said one of the dwarfs. "I expect you are hungry. Come. Sit down. Tell us your name. Tell us how you came to be here."

The dwarfs were so good humoured that Snow White did as they said. She told them that her stepmother had plotted to kill her, but the huntsman had let her go.

"You still haven't told us your name," they said.

"I'm called Snow White," she answered, adding that she was the daughter of a king.

"And what is your age?" asked the dwarfs, astonished that a princess should be abandoned in this way.

Snow White tried to think. "I'm not sure," she said, "but the last time I had a birthday I was seven years old. I had no more after that."

The dwarfs gasped in astonishment – for the girl who sat before them looked at least thirteen years of age.

"But how did you get here?" they asked. "There are seven mountains between our cottage and your palace."

"I don't know," said Snow White. "It is all so much like a dream. Like endless night. Wild animals showed me the way."

"It is a mystery," said the dwarfs. "But we must be thankful for that. At least you are safe here. If you take care of our house, cook, make the beds, wash and brush, dust and polish, sew and knit, and keep everything neat and tidy, you can stay with us and want for nothing."

"Gladly," said Snow White. "This is such a dear little house that I think I should enjoy taking care of it."

So it was agreed.

The next morning, when the dwarfs were setting off for the mountains, they had something else to say. "There is one thing more. Beware! Your stepmother will soon find out where you are and she may come in search of you. Be sure to let no one in while we are away. And be sure to stay indoors."

"May I not even gather food from the garden?" asked Snow White.

"Not even that," said the dwarfs. "We will fetch all that is needed."

After they had gone Snow White spent a long time looking out of the window at the grass, the flowers, the sky. "At least I may lean out once in a while," she said to herself, "and breathe in the sweet fresh air." Then she settled down to her work.

The Queen was no fool. She knew that with so many ugly feelings raging inside her she would not be very beautiful, despite the pampering of her maids. So she put on a show of sorrow for the King whenever he mentioned the loss of Snow White, soothing him and weeping such tears that she almost believed in them herself. "What a tragic queen I am," she thought. "How fine I look in my mourning clothes. How everyone must pity me."

When she felt quite sure that her wickedness was buried deep down she went once again to the magic mirror:

"Mirror, mirror, on the wall,

Who is the fairest one of all?"

The mirror answered:

"You, O Queen, are wondrous fair,

But with beauty still more rare

Snow White is living, safe and well

By a greenwood tree, where seven dwarfs dwell."

The Queen was furious at this! Her eyes blazed and her hair fizzed. She knew that the mirror never lied. So Snow White had escaped and the huntsman had betrayed her. "Brat!" she snarled. "Traitor!"

She brooded and plotted, prowling and scowling. She would not rest until once again she was the fairest in the land. How could she be rid of Snow White?

Now the Queen was well practised in the black arts and soon concocted an evil plan. She took two snakes and turned them into laces. Then she stained her face grey and disguised herself as an old pedlar woman. No one would have known her. Pretending to have a crooked back, she set out on a journey over seven mountains in search of Snow White.

Not for her the struggle of winding paths, the rocky slopes, the treacherous precipices. Oh, no. Using her sorcery she had made a pair of magic slippers that could take her anywhere she wanted to go without effort. Hobbledy-hop, hobbledy-hop over seven mountains she went, until she reached the home of the seven dwarfs. She knocked on the door and cried, "Good day, little maid. Spare some water for a poor old woman."

When Snow White heard her voice she stopped still and listened.

She knew what the dwarfs had told her: speak to no one; listen to no one; admit no one. But they had only warned her about a wicked queen, not a poor old woman begging for a drink of water. How could she refuse? She opened the casement window just a crack and called, "There is water in the well. You may help yourself."

"Why, thank you, little one," said the Queen. "What a sweet voice you have. I expect you are very pretty. Come. Show me your face. See what I have in my basket."

Snow White's curiosity grew. She opened the casement window a little further and peeped outside. There stood an old pedlar woman on the veranda, with a gleaming basket of ribbons and lace. What could be the harm?

The old woman grinned. "Oh, how pretty you are indeed. I have pretty things for a pretty girl. Very fine. Very cheap."

The truth is, Snow White was finding it mighty hard work to be housekeeper to seven dwarfs. Every day there were seven beds to make, seven plates and seven goblets to wash, seven tunics to be scrubbed and ironed, seven pairs of boots to be polished. There was a mountain of socks to wash and sort, because it was dusty work in the mines. There was copper to polish and glass to shine. There was a grate to be cleaned and floors to be swept, for the dwarfs liked everything to be spick and span. Then there were seven suppers to cook. And she was not even allowed to step into the fresh air of the garden.

Snow White was a princess, hardly out of her childhood, and although she did everything as cheerfully and as well as she could, she was not used to such labour. There was no girlish frippery in the dwarfs' house, no frills or feminine finery. Why, she did not even have a change of clothes for herself!

The old woman spoke again. "Pretty things for a pretty girl. Who will buy from a poor old woman? Tell your fortune, pretty girl. Come, show me your palm."

Forgetting all that she had been told, she opened the window wider and offered her hand. "Very well, old woman," said Snow White. "Show me what you have in your basket."

The old woman seized her hand and pretended to read her palm. "Oh, I see a happy ending for you," she snickered, adding under her breath, "and sooner than you think!" With that, she pulled out two long silken laces and let their shining colours stream through her bony fingers.

"Laces," she said. "Lovely long laces for your bodice. Cheap. Very cheap. Come, take a good look."

This was too much for Snow White. She unbolted the door. No sooner had she done so than the old woman sprang inside.

"My, what a sight you look," said the old woman. "Come, let me lace you up."

Snow White was a trusting person. There was no mirror in the dwarfs' house but she knew that after all her housework she probably looked like a kitchenmaid. So she let the old woman thread the laces through her bodice and tie them together. "Breathe in," urged the sly crone, "breathe in."

The deadly laces did their work. Tighter and tighter they squeezed Snow White until she could breathe no more. Her eyelids fluttered, her lips trembled, her limbs went slack. At last she dropped down as if dead.

"Hah! That will teach you," said the wicked Queen. "So much for vanity! So much for your beauty, too! Now let us see who is fairest."

Prodding Snow White with her slipper to make sure she was dead, the Queen slithered out of the door.

When the dwarfs returned that evening to find Snow White as still as stone on the ground, they were full of sorrow and dismay. They lifted her gently and seeing how tightly she was laced, they immediately untied her bodice. But instead of laces on the ground, there were bits of snake that wriggled and coiled until they were dead.

Snow White started to breathe again. Her eyes opened wide. "What happened?" she said. "Where am I?" Then she recalled the old pedlar woman and told the dwarfs what had happened.

"That was no pedlar," said one of the dwarfs. "See this!" And he held up a single strand of burnished copper hair he had found on a bush by the door. "That was your wicked stepmother! She will be back, that's for sure. You must take care. Speak to no one; listen to no one; admit no one."

That evening they tried to soothe Snow White by making their own supper and by singing songs and telling stories of the mountains and mines where they worked.

Hobbledy-hop, hobbledy-hop went the wicked Queen over seven mountains, until she was back at the palace. As soon as she was rid of her disguise and had smoothed herself down, she went gleefully to the magic mirror and asked,

"Mirror, mirror, on the wall,

Who is the fairest one of all?"

The mirror answered:

"You have beauty, Queen, 'tis true

But lovelier by far than you

Breathes another, darkly bright,

Her name you know: it is Snow White!"

What a rage possessed the Queen. She bubbled and boiled. She frothed and foamed. She sizzled and spat.

"Hah!" she cried. "I won't fail next time. I will put an end to that wretched creature if it's the last thing I do!"

Soon she had hatched another cunning plan. She took a poisonous black spider and, using her tricks, she turned it into a beautiful comb, made of jet and inlaid with mother of pearl.

For a second time she disguised herself as an old woman. Again she put on her magic slippers and travelled over seven mountains, scribble-scrabble, scribble-scrabble, sideways like a crab, until she reached the house of the seven dwarfs.

Snow White sat sewing. She had a basket of socks to darn, she had seven shirts needing new buttons, seven pairs of trousers needing patches. There was broth to be made and bread to be baked. She sighed and dreamed of summer in the palace garden.

A knock at the door interrupted her thoughts. And then a voice:

"Fine things. Trinkets. Bangles. Baubles. Come! See what I have for sale."

Ah! Snow White had listened. She sat in terrified silence for a while, hoping the person would go away.

"Fine things," cooed the voice. "Come on.

I know you're there."

Snow White spoke. She simply could not help it. "Go away!" she said. "I cannot let anyone in."

"Come, my dear," said the voice. "There can be no harm in taking a look."

What a silken, velvet voice! What soothing subtlety in the offer it made. Snow White loved the seven dwarfs and they were kind to her, but she missed the chatter and laughter of the women who used to attend her, and all her fine things. A peep. Just one little peep.

Snow White opened the door a crack. There stood an old woman with an enticing smile on her face. Before Snow White had time to protest, the creature pushed the door wider ajar.

"What a mess your hair is, child!" she exclaimed. "Do you never comb it? Why, it is as tangled as a holly bush." She held up the jet comb. "See this comb. This is no ordinary comb. One touch and your tangles fall away. One stroke and it will undo your knots. With this comb your beautiful black hair will always be smooth and shining. Come, let me—"

And before Snow White could close the door, the old woman started to comb her long black hair. The poison did its work immediately and Snow White fell down in a swoon of death.

"Eh, eh!" cackled the Queen. "So much for your fine tresses. Now let us see who is the most beautiful of all."

And she danced a triumphant jig around Snow White's body, before scuttling out of the door.

At dusk the seven dwarfs returned home. They were looking forward to a good supper. How they loved having Snow White to come home to, with the place so cosy and welcoming. How shocked they were when they found her still and lifeless on the ground once again. They raised her head and immediately the jet comb fell out of her hair. It turned back into a spider and scurried away.

Snow White opened her eyes. She told the dwarfs about the old woman who had come to the door.

"How could you be so foolish?" said the smallest dwarf. "That was no ordinary old woman. That was your stepmother. That was no ordinary comb. Look at this," and he picked out a silver thread that the spider had spun in Snow White's hair.

"But she seemed so kind," protested Snow White. "Not a bit like my stepmother."

"She has wicked means to achieve her wicked ends," said the dwarfs. "She knows how to hide her intent. You must remember what we say. Trust absolutely no one who comes to the door, no matter what they seem. Promise."

"I promise," said Snow White, shuddering at the thought of the spider.

"Don't worry about the spider," said the dwarfs. "That horror has gone looking for its owner. Now come, let us make supper together and be of good cheer."

When the Queen arrived home she washed herself and changed her garments. Then she brushed her fiery copper hair and painted her face, before turning to her mirror:

"Mirror, mirror, on the wall,
Who is the fairest one of all?"

The mirror answered:

"O cruel Queen, why do you ask?
Your beauty now is but a mask.
Fair of face, with heart as true,
Snow White is lovelier far than you."

The Queen's heart knocked in her ribcage. She could hardly contain her rage. She writhed and itched. She wriggled and twitched. She was in such a fit of rage and so contorted that she resembled nothing so much as a black and poisonous spider herself. She scuttled away into a dark corner to hatch a far more dangerous plot. "I will finish her next time, once and for all," she snarled.

Like a shadow she brooded in her secret room, giving herself no rest.

Then she came up with her deadliest plot. She chose a delicious-looking apple, round and red on one side, yellow on the other. The red side she injected with the poisonous sting of a scorpion. Whoever looked on it would long for it; whoever tasted it would be sure to die.

Once again she stained her face, disguising herself as a simple countrywoman, and set off in her magic slippers over seven mountains for the home of the seven dwarfs. She slithered and slid, skimmed and skipped, until she arrived at the veranda of the wooden house.

Inside, Snow White was in a daydream. She was preparing supper for the dwarfs: bone broth and vegetable stew. She had simmered and stirred the bones, and peeled and chopped the vegetables. They were still using their winter store: knobbly swedes and turnips, hairy carrots and parsnips, potatoes with a hundred eyes, mushy peas. To these she added roots, dried beans, pulses, cured bacon, rindy cheese. Although she did her best to make it tasty with herbs and spices, this was dwarf food, coarse and rough, to keep stomachs warm underground. Snow White was used to princess food, far daintier fare. How she longed for something fresh: a sprig of parsley perhaps, a cherry, a strawberry . . . maybe even an apple.

Her mouth watered at the thought.

Suddenly there was a knock at the door. "Apples. Juicy ripe apples. Who will buy my apples?"

Without thinking, Snow White spoke. "Go away. I am to listen to no one, speak to no one, admit no one."

But once again came the soft and honeyed voice, full of temptation. "See my apples. Smell my apples. Taste my lovely, luscious apples."

Such a wily, beguiling voice. It stole straight into Snow White's senses, almost as though she were hypnotised. Like a sleepwalker, she went to the window, turned the catch and opened it just a slit.

"Here," said the old woman, thrusting an apple under her nose. "Smell it. Try one. Ripe, round, juicy red apples."

"No," Snow White managed to say, "I am forbidden."

"I see you are suspicious," said the old woman. "Perhaps you think that this apple is not so good as it looks. Perhaps you think it is rotten in the centre, with a maggot! Have no fear. I will show you. See! I will eat the yellow half. You may have the red. This is no ordinary apple, I can tell you. This apple has all the tastes of paradise."

When Snow White saw that the old woman had come to no harm when she ate the yellow half, she could resist no longer. She stretched out her hand and took the poisonous red half of the apple. Just as promised, the apple looked good and wholesome to the core. But hardly had she bitten into it than the poison did its work and she fell down dead.

The Queen skipped round Snow White's lifeless body. She kicked her heels. She yelped for joy. "Hah!" she cackled. "White as death, red as rage, black as the pit of my heart. Nothing the dwarfs can do will save you now."

Then she slithered and skimmed back over the mountains. She was sure that Snow White was finally dead and that the mirror would tell her what she wanted to hear.

Even so, she was taking no chances. "Come," she said to her seven maids, "Let me look my most beautiful." They bathed her in milk and polished her hair with silk. They dressed her in the finest robes and adorned her with the richest jewels. When they had finished, the Queen stood before her magic mirror and asked,

"Mirror, mirror, on the wall,

Who is the fairest one of all?"

The mirror gleamed and winked, as though it were itself bedazzled. Then it answered,

"Over the mountains, dead and gone,

Lies a maid whose beauty shone.

To match you now, O Queen, there's none.

You reign supreme, the fairest one."

The Queen smiled her cold glittering smile. Her jealous heart could rest at last – in so far as a jealous heart can rest. The mirror could only speak the truth. Ah! But what is truth? Despite her ugly feelings and ugly deeds, the glass reflected only her beauty.

When the dwarfs came home in the evening they found Snow White still and lifeless on the ground once again. They loosened her laces and searched her hair to see if there were any poisonous things about her. They found none. They held a piece of crystal before her mouth to see if there was breath. There was none.

They washed her in water and wine, but it was no use. She was dead, and remained dead, and they could not revive her.

"We can't have lost her forever," said one of the dwarfs.

"She was so full of life," said another.

"It's our own fault," said a third. "We should never have left her alone."

"She should have listened to us," said a fourth. "If only she had heeded our warning."

"She was lonely," said a fifth. "And so young and trusting."

"We asked too much of her," said a sixth.

"She will never come again," said a seventh.

But they could not believe that this was the end of her story.

They laid her upon a bier strewn with flowers and smoothed out her beautiful black hair. For three days and nights they wept by her bedside.

They were going to bury her, but they noticed that her lips were still red, her cheeks, though pale, still glowed and her hair had lost none of its lustre.

"We cannot bury her in the dark ground," they said. So they made a beautiful glass casket and underneath in gold letters they inscribed:

Softly draw near ⁓ Snow White lies here
⁓ She was the daughter of a king ⁓
⁓ Now sleeps she under death's dark wing ⁓

They carried the casket to an icy mountain peak, so inaccessible that only they could find the way. One at a time they kept watch over it, together with the moon and stars. Birds came too. First an owl, with a red rose in its beak, then a raven, which left a black feather, and last a dove, which left a white feather.

Three years passed. The dwarfs kept watch over Snow White's glassy coffin. Although they went on toiling in the mountains, they had lost all their joy in life. Snow White remained as beautiful as ever, frozen in time, just as she was on the day she had died.

One day, a prince who was hunting in the forest outpaced all of his huntsmen in chasing a fawn. Suddenly the fawn turned to face the Prince, completely unafraid. Such soft doe eyes it had, such gentle grace. He could not bring himself to kill such a creature. The fawn seemed to beckon and the Prince followed, until to his amazement he came to a little wooden house in a clearing, where seven lanterns glowed from seven windows.

Night was beginning to fall and the Prince had no hope of finding his companions. Perhaps whoever lived here would give him shelter.

When the Prince knocked on the door, the dwarfs were as welcoming as ever, but the same was not true of their house. Sadness hung in cobwebs, sorrow trailed in the dust. The Prince was a sensitive soul and he could tell something was wrong. "What misfortune has there been here?" he asked the dwarfs.

In answer they pointed to the casket gleaming on the mountain peak like a distant diamond. Then they told the Prince their story.

"Take me to the coffin," he begged. "Let me look upon Snow White."

"It isn't as easy as that," said the dwarfs. "Whoever reaches her must find his own way. And the way is steep and treacherous. Many a man has perished on those slopes, fallen down a gulley, slid off a precipice."

Even so, the Prince set out. For seven days he journeyed, at times freezing cold, often losing his foothold so that he would have to go over the same ground again. But he knew that this was his destiny, that he had no choice but to go on. For a prize so rare as a glimpse of this princess, enchanted in her dream of death, he knew that the price was high. At last he reached the coffin.

When he saw Snow White lying there he realised that this was the maiden he had always loved, before he knew her face or name.

"Let me have the coffin," he begged the dwarf who was keeping watch. "I will pay a king's ransom for her."

But the dwarfs would not hear of it. "What use to us is gold?" they said. "What need do we have of jewels? We have all the riches we want in the world. She is worth more than all that to us."

"Then give her to me," said the Prince. "I will honour and prize her above anyone else. I shall build a monument to house her casket that shall be a wonder of the world. She shall be dearer to my heart than anyone living."

Still the dwarfs refused. "Then I shall stay by her side until I, too, am dead," said the Prince.

After three days, when they saw how he peaked and pined, the dwarfs relented. After all, it was more fitting that a princess should lie in the grounds of a palace instead of on a bleak and lonely mountain.

The Prince had to make the gruelling journey yet again, only this time with his servants. Then slowly, step by step, they began to bring the coffin down the mountain.

They had not gone far when they stumbled on a sharp ridge. For one terrible moment it seemed that they might let the coffin slide down

a crevasse, never to be seen again. With every nerve in his body, every fibre of his being, the Prince held on, until the coffin was secure once again. But the jolt had shaken its precious cargo. No longer did Snow White seem so still. The Prince gazed in disbelief as a tiny tremor went through her body. What was this? A miracle? "She stirs! The Princess stirs!" he cried. There was a gulp, a cough, a struggle for breath, then Snow White opened her eyes!

The Prince leapt to her side and gently raised the coffin lid

"What happened?" said Snow White, staring at the wide blue sky above her and the shining mountain peaks all around. "Where am I?"

Mercifully, Snow White had not swallowed the poisonous piece of apple. It had been stuck all this while in her throat and now was dislodged. She felt herself warmed by the lambent gaze of clear grey eyes and the gentlest human touch. "Who are you?" she sighed.

The Prince gazed and gazed at her. Now that she had regained the beauty of life, he could see the depth of beauty within.

"One who loves you most in all the world," said the Prince, raising her up. "Come with me to my father's palace and be my bride."

Snow White had never seen such a wondrous creature as this Prince. Gladly she went with him to his palace, with the seven dwarfs and the Prince's retinue in attendance, and the couple were betrothed.

A splendid wedding was arranged. A thousand guests were invited and all over the land there were celebrations. Snow White wore a veil of lace like a gentle fall of snow. On her feet she wore black silken slippers and around her neck there hung a single red ruby given to her by the dwarfs.

Rulers came from far and wide, including Snow White's father and stepmother. The Queen had heard about the beautiful new princess and her heart was already inflamed and plotting.

When she was dressed and coiffured and bejewelled, she stood before her magic mirror:

"Mirror, mirror on the wall,

Who is the fairest one of all?"

A swirling mist appeared in the mirror, then a deep pool of water. At last the mirror spoke:

"In me you have your beauty drowned;

A new queen will be fairest crowned.

Beware! O wicked Queen, beware!

The face you have deserved you'll wear."

The evil creature cursed and spat. She gnashed her teeth and tore at her hair until it was a crown of snarls. No one could mistake now the cruel lines around her mouth and the savage frown on her brow, not even the Queen herself. She saw them with hideous clarity. With a terrible screech she smashed the magic mirror, so that it shattered into a thousand pieces.

Now, almost as ugly on the outside as she was on the inside, she was tortured by the thought of this new queen. She had to go and see this fresh usurper, even though it was a torment.

No procession was grander than the Queen's, no train more magnificent, no veil more concealing than the one she was obliged to wear. But it was all to no avail. There to welcome her, in stunning, splendid simplicity, was the bride. When the Queen saw that she was none other than her hated stepdaughter, Snow White, now grown up to be a beautiful woman, she ripped off her veil in a rage and stood there, rooted to the spot. The King looked on in dismay. Who was this creature that stood before him, this hideous gorgon? What had happened to his exquisite queen?

Even more amazed was Snow White, when she saw this king who had come to her wedding. "Father," she said. "Don't you know me?"

Confused and overwhelmed, her father looked from his wife to his daughter, from his daughter to his wife. The scales fell from his eyes. For the first time he saw his wife as she really was, a boiling cauldron of jealousy and spite.

But what tears of joy when he realised that this was Snow White, that she was indeed alive! What tears of anger when he heard what the Queen had done! "I was told you had been torn apart by wolves in the forest. A huntsman paid with his life for his neglect. O wicked cruel creature! I have been like one bewitched. Look at the foul fiend! She shall surely be punished."

But the Queen's punishment was of her own making. All the burning hatred and jealousy she had felt for so long went out of her heart and down to her feet until her magic slippers were red hot. Her evil now exposed for all to see, the Queen's rage turned to fear. She tried to run, to fly, to flee, but her magic slippers did not help her now. She struggled

to hop, to scrabble, to slide, but could only squirm.

Then, oh my, what a dreadful sight to behold. The slippers seared and scalded, shocking her feet into action. And then, how she danced! She did the dance of seven snakes, seven spiders, seven scorpions, sizzling in her own spite. Around her head her burnished copper hair blazed like a fire and her forest-green eyes became smouldering black coals. Her flawless olive skin was like peeling bark as she danced a terrible dance of death

Then it was over. Nothing remained of the Queen but a pile of ashes, and peace and harmony were restored. As Snow White and her prince did the dance of love into the future, bells rang, flags unfurled, and fireworks lit up the sky. The stars danced too, twinkling with promise and hope.

The King asked his daughter for forgiveness and, ever after, on the seventh day of the seventh month, the dwarfs were invited to a banquet. Snow White saw to it herself that all was laid as neatly and smoothly and brightly as it was in their cottage and that they had plentiful helpings of dwarf food, as well as all the

splendid royal delicacies.

The happiness of the royal couple spread throughout the land. With such a brave king and a wise queen on the throne, the kingdom prospered as never before.

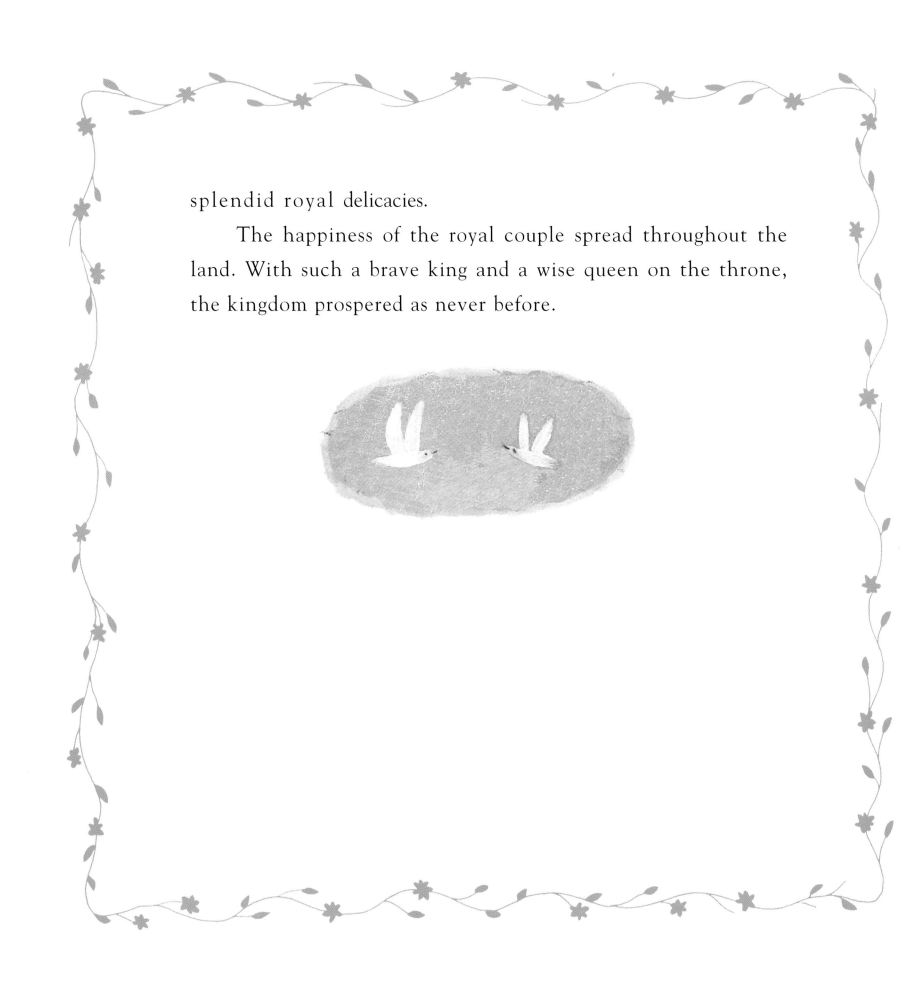

Once a year, on a winter's night, a beautiful woman was seen to visit two graves. One belonged to her mother, the other to her stepmother. On both, Snow White placed a red rose, a black feather and a white feather. For both women she felt pity. And shining in her soul was a perception far clearer than any mirror can show: that the only true beauty is the goodness of the heart.

The End